D0585808

This LADYBIRD CLASSIC
belongs to

....

A History of the Author

Kenneth Grahame was born in Edinburgh in 1859. He wrote many books and essays, but in 1908, when *The Wind in the Willows* was published, he was working as a secretary in the Bank of England. The book is based on bedtime stories he made up for his young son. Grahame died on 6th July 1932.

Chapter illustrations by Valeria Valenza

A catalogue record for this book is available from the British Library

Published by Ladybird Books Ltd
80 Strand London WC2R 0RL
A Penguin Company

006

© Ladybird Books Ltd MMXIII

LADYBIRD and the device of a Ladybird are trademarks of Ladybird Books Ltd

All rights reserved. No part of this publication may be reproduced, stored in a retrieval system, or transmitted in any form or by any means, electronic, mechanical, photocopying, recording or otherwise, without the prior consent of the copyright owner.

ISBN: 978-1-40931-356-4

Printed in China

LADYBIRD  CLASSICS

THE WIND IN THE WILLOWS

by Kenneth Grahame

Retold by Joan Collins
Illustrated by Ester García-Cortés

Contents

CHAPTER ONE

The River Bank

THE MOLE HAD been working very hard all morning, spring-cleaning his little home. There were splashes of whitewash all over his black fur. His back ached and his arms were tired.

It was spring in the world outside. Mole could feel the fresh air and sunshine calling to him in the dark, underground burrow.

Suddenly he threw his brush down.

'Bother!' he said. 'Oh, blow!' he said. 'Hang spring-cleaning!' He bolted out of the house and scrambled up the steep, narrow tunnel that was his front entrance.

He had to scrape and scratch and scrabble with his little paws, muttering to himself, 'Up we go! Up we go!' At last – *pop!* – his snout came out into the sunlight, and he found himself rolling in the warm grass of a great meadow.

'This is fine! This is better than whitewashing!' he said as he bounded joyfully across the meadow.

Suddenly he came to the bank of a river. He had never seen a river before. The water was full of life and movement, glints and gleams and sparkles. Mole trotted beside it, fascinated, until he was tired out.

He sat down on the grassy bank and listened to the sound of the water. As he looked at the opposite bank, he saw a

dark hole. Something bright and small twinkled in it. It winked, and he saw it was an eye! Then a small face appeared.

A brown little face with whiskers.

Small neat ears and thick silky hair.

It was the Water Rat!

The animals stood and looked at each other.

'Hello, Mole!' said the Water Rat.

'Hello, Rat!' said the Mole.

'Would you like to come over?'

'How can I get to you?' said Mole, not knowing the ways of the river.

The Rat stooped down and unfastened a rope. He hauled up a little blue and white boat, just the size for two animals. He rowed across, and gave Mole his paw, to step down timidly into it.

The two animals made friends at once. Ratty was very surprised to hear that Mole had never been in a boat before.

'There is *nothing* half so much worth

doing,' he told Mole, 'as simply messing
about in boats.'

Then he had an idea. 'If you've really
nothing else to do this morning, why
don't we go down the river together
and make a long day of it?'

'Let's start at once!' said Mole, settling
back happily into the soft cushions.

The Rat fetched a wicker picnic
basket. 'Shove that under your feet!'

'What's inside?' asked Mole.

'There's cold chicken,' said Rat,
'coldtonguecoldhamcoldbeefpickledonions
saladfrenchbreadcresssandwidgespotted
meatgingerbeerlemonade –'

'Oh stop!' cried Mole in ecstasy. 'This
is *too* much!'

'Do you think so?' said Rat seriously.
'It's only what I always take on these
little outings.'

Rat rowed silently down the river,
while Mole took in all the new sights,

smells and sounds. The Water Rat enjoyed
his friend's pleasure and explained he
loved the river so.

'It's my world and I don't want
any other.'

'But isn't it a bit dull at times?'
asked Mole. 'Just you and the river,
and nobody else?'

'Nobody else! You must be joking!
It's full of people – too many of them
sometimes – otters, moorhens, ducks and
so on, about all day long!'

'What lies over *there*?' asked Mole,
waving a paw towards a dark background
of woodland beyond the fields.

'Oh, that's just the Wild Wood. We don't
go there much, we riverbankers.'

'Aren't they – very nice people in
there?' asked Mole nervously.

'Well – the squirrels are all right. The
rabbits are a mixed lot. And Badger's all
right. But there *are* others – weasels and

stoats, and foxes and so on. All right
in a way. But you can't trust them.'

'And beyond the Wild Wood? Where
it's all blue and dim and there's hills – and
something like the smoke from towns?'

'Beyond the Wild Wood comes the
Wide World,' said the Rat, 'and that's
something that doesn't matter to you
or me.'

So Rat and Mole began their picnic.
While they were eating, they met two
of Rat's friends. One was the Otter,
swimming underwater to catch fish. He
climbed out on the bank, shook himself
and had a word with them. Drops of
water glistened on his whiskers.

The other was Mr Badger, whose
stripy head suddenly pushed through
the thorny hedge. He grunted, 'Hm!
Company!' and disappeared.

Mr Toad was on the river too – he
shot past in a brand-new racing skiff.

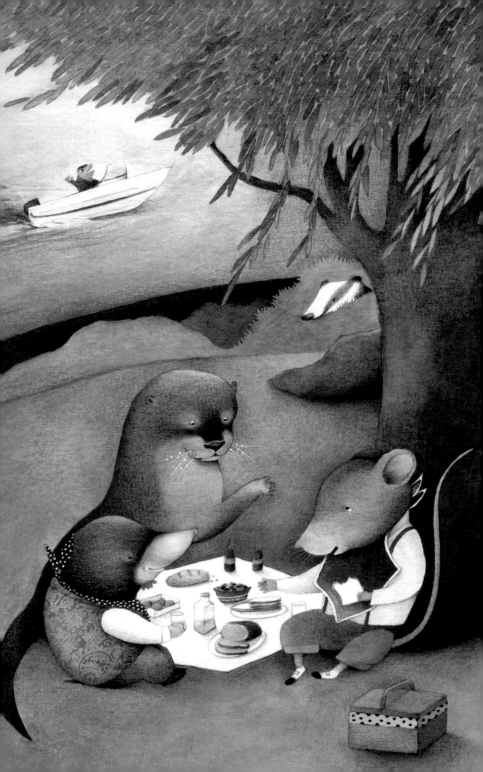

He was short and fat, splashing badly and rolling from side to side.

'He'll never do well in a boat,' said Rat.

'Not steady enough,' said Otter, and suddenly vanished after a fish.

'Toad's always trying something new,' explained Rat. 'Last year he had a houseboat. But he soon gets tired of things.'

Rat and Mole went back to Rat's snug home in the river bank and sat in armchairs beside a bright fire, chatting. Rat invited Mole to stay with him for the rest of the summer. The happy Mole went to sleep in a comfy bedroom. His newly found friend, the river, was lapping against the bank below his windowsill, and he could hear the wind, whispering in the willows.

CHAPTER TWO

The Open Road

NEXT DAY, THE Water Rat took
Mole to visit Mr Toad, who lived
nearby in a handsome house called
Toad Hall. It was built of mellow red
brick and had lawns reaching down
to the river.

Toad was rather rich, but not a very
sensible animal. Ratty and Badger
had to keep an eye on him. He was

good-natured, but inclined to show off, and he was always getting into trouble.

The friends found him sitting in a deck-chair in the garden, looking at a road map. He had bought a gipsy caravan, painted bright yellow with green trim and red wheels. There was an old grey horse to draw it. Toad was planning to take his first trip that afternoon, and he persuaded Mole and Rat to go along with him.

Toad was bouncing about, full of the joys of the open road – its freedom and fresh air. 'Here today and somewhere else tomorrow! Across the rolling downs!' he cried excitedly.

The three of them set out but, before they had gone very far, disaster struck! They were walking along the country lane quite happily, leading the horse. Suddenly a loud *Poop! Poop!* was heard.

A magnificent motor car, all plate glass and chromium, flashed past them, flinging out a cloud of blinding dust. Then it was gone, a speck in the distance.

The poor horse was frightened and bolted. The caravan turned over and fell into the ditch. Its windows were smashed, and one wheel came off.

Ratty and Mole were furious. 'You road hog!' they shouted, shaking their fists. But Toad just sat there in the dust, a dazed look in his eyes, muttering, '*Poop! Poop!*' He did not care about the wrecked caravan. He was already thinking how marvellous it would be to drive a car.

Next day, on the river bank, everyone was talking about the latest news.

'Have you heard? Toad went up to London by an early train this morning. And he has ordered – what do you think? – a large and very expensive *motor car*!'

Chapter Three

The Wild Wood

THE LONG, HOT summer had ended
at last. Now it was winter. Mole was still
staying with Ratty, on the river bank.

One cold afternoon, the Mole decided
to go to the Wild Wood and visit Mr
Badger. He was the only one of Rat's
friends that the Mole had not met
properly, as he was not very sociable.
In the winter, most animals stay at home

and rest, after an active summer. Some
of them go to sleep for most of the time,
and you cannot persuade them to do
very much.

So Mole knew that if he wanted to see
Mr Badger he would have to call on him.

He slipped out of Ratty's warm
parlour into the open air. The sky was
steely. The countryside was bare. Twigs
crackled under Mole's feet. Trees took on
ugly, crouching shapes. The light faded.
Mole began to feel frightened.

Then the scary faces began to emerge
– little, evil, wedge-shaped faces, looking
out of holes and then vanishing. Mole
kept up his pace and, looking round,
saw every hole with a face in it, all fixing
him with evil, sharp looks.

Then the whistling began. Very faint
and shrill, behind and then ahead of him.
Mole was alone, and far from help, and
night was closing in.

Then the pattering began. Tiny feet pursuing him, rustling through the fallen leaves. He ran and started bumping into trees.

Meanwhile, Rat had discovered Mole was not at home. He saw his footprints outside, leading to the Wild Wood. Seizing a stout stick, he set out at a smart pace to track him. At last he found the Mole in the shelter of an old beech tree, trembling all over and so glad his friend had come.

And then it began to snow, thick and fast. Soon a white carpet covered the ground, and all the paths and landmarks were lost.

Rat and Mole made their way with difficulty through the Wild Wood. Then Mole fell against something hard that cut his leg. It was a door-scraper.

'Where there's a door-scraper, there must be a door!' said Ratty sensibly. Digging down, they found a doormat,

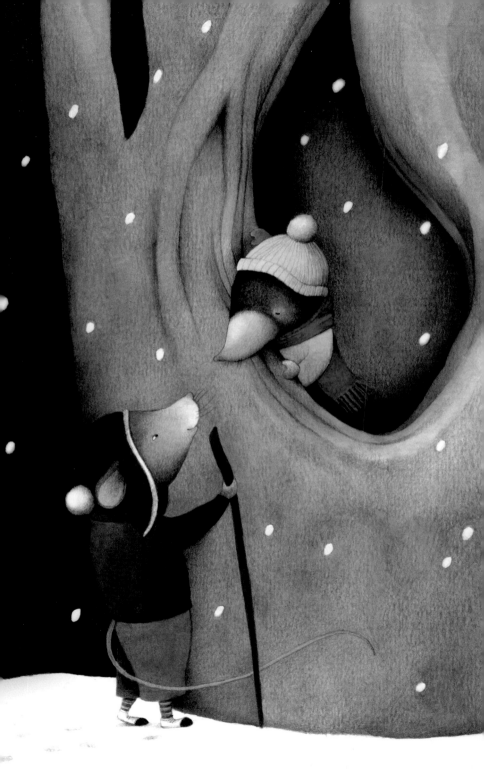

and then a very solid front door, with
a brass plate with 'MR BADGER' on it,
and an old-fashioned bell pull. They
tugged at it.

They could hear the bell clanging
a long way down. Badger took some
time to come to the door, wearing his
old slippers and a thick dressing gown.
He was rather grumpy at first at being
disturbed, but welcomed them into his
firelit kitchen.

Great smoked hams and strings of
fat brown onions hung from the rafters
overhead. Badger gave them a good
supper, and they sat talking by the fire
about Toad and his craze for motor cars.
'Something will have to be done about
that,' said Badger, 'when the winter
is over.'

In the morning, they had porridge
for breakfast, with two young hedgehogs
who had got lost on their way to school.

Badger showed them all the back door out of his lair, through a maze of tunnels that led to the edge of the wood.

Looking back, Mole and Rat saw the Wild Wood, black, threatening and grim against the snow, and made their way quickly home, safe once more on the friendly river bank.

CHAPTER FOUR

Home Sweet Home

IT WAS ALMOST Christmas. Mole
and Rat had been out exploring the
countryside. It was getting dark when
they passed through a country village.
Firelight and lamplight shone in the
windows. They could see children being
put to bed, a man knocking out his pipe
on a smouldering log and, in one window,
the shadow of a bird cage, with a sleepy

bird ruffled up in its feathers. They felt tired, cold and lonely, and far from home.

The two animals plodded on across the fields. Mole was following Rat, his nose to the ground. As he sniffed, he felt a tingle, like an electric shock. Animals can pick up signals from smells that humans never notice. This particular smell meant *home* to Mole.

In the excitement of his new life, Mole had forgotten his own little home. But now it all came back to him, and he called to Ratty to stop.

But Ratty did not hear, and cried, 'Oh, come on, Mole! Don't hang behind! We've a long way to go!'

Poor Mole stood alone in the road. He wanted so badly to follow the scent, but he could not desert his friend. He struggled on, slowly.

Soon Ratty noticed how quiet his friend was and how he was dragging his feet. Then he heard a sniff and a stifled sob, and it all came out.

'I know it's only a shabby little place,' sobbed Mole, 'not like your cosy home, or Toad Hall. But it was my own and I was fond of it.'

Ratty patted his shoulder. 'What a selfish pig I've been,' he thought. And he turned Mole round and they set off back the way they had come, to pick up the scent.

At last, after several false starts, Mole crossed a ditch, scrambled through a hedge and dived down a tunnel. At the end of it was a little front door with 'MOLE END' painted on it. Mole lit a lantern and they could see a neat forecourt with a garden seat, some hanging baskets with ferns, and a plaster bust of Queen Victoria.

There was a skittle alley, too, and a goldfish pond with a cockleshell border.

Inside, everything was dusty and rather shabby. Mole started to sniff again, ashamed at having brought his friend there. But Ratty ran to and fro, lighting lamps and candles, exploring rooms and cupboards. He started to light a fire, while Mole got busy with a duster.

'What a capital little house this is!' Rat called out cheerfully. 'So compact and well planned!'

'But I haven't got anything for supper!' Mole wailed.

'Rubbish!' said the Rat. 'I spy a sardine tin opener, so there must be some sardines.' They found some biscuits and were just about to open the sardines when there was a scuffling noise in the forecourt, a lot of coughing and a murmur of tiny voices.

'What's that?' asked Rat.

'It must be the field mice,' answered Mole. 'They go round this time of year, carol-singing.'

They opened the door, and there, in the light of a lantern, eight or ten little field mice stood in a semicircle.

They wore red knitted scarves round their necks, and they jigged up and down to keep their feet warm.

'One, two, three!' cried the eldest one, and their shrill, tiny voices rose in an old-time carol about the animals in the stable at Bethlehem.

'Who were the first to cry Nowell?
Animals all, as it befell,
In the stable where they did dwell!
Joy shall be theirs in the morning!'

Just as they finished, the sound of distant church bells came floating down the tunnel.

Mole and Rat welcomed the little carol-singers in, and Ratty sent one of them off with a basket and some money to buy food. The rest of the mice sat on a bench by the fire and warmed their chilblains, drinking mugs of hot punch. When the messenger returned, they had a splendid supper.

They finally clattered off home, with presents for their families. Mole and Rat tucked themselves into bed in handy sleeping bunks. Before he closed his eyes, Mole looked happily about his old room in the glow of the firelight.

Thanks to his friend's kindness, Mole's pleasure in his old home had returned. 'Everyone needs a place of his own to come back to,' he thought drowsily, before he dropped off to sleep.

CHAPTER FIVE

Mr Toad

ONE BRIGHT MORNING in early
summer, Badger kept his promise to
visit Ratty and Mole.

'It's time we did something about
Toad,' he grunted. 'He's a disgrace to
the neighbourhood. What my old friend,
his father, would have said about his
doings, I don't like to think. This craze
for motor cars is getting him into trouble
with the police!'

'Yes, he's had several crashes,' agreed Rat. 'I hear he has ordered another new car this week.'

They set off for Toad Hall. Sure enough, there at the front door stood a shiny, brand-new, bright red motor car. Mr Toad, in goggles, cap, gaiters and a huge overcoat came swaggering down the steps, putting on his big leather driving gloves.

'You're just in time for a jolly spin, you fellows!' he called out cheerfully.

'Oh, no, you don't!' said Badger gruffly, seizing him by the scruff of the neck and marching him back into the house. Mole and Rat took off his ridiculous motoring togs, and Badger gave him a good talking-to.

Toad refused to promise to give up driving, so they locked him in his bedroom to think it over.

But cunning Toad pretended to be ill and, while they were fetching the doctor, he skipped out of the window and bounced

off to the village, laughing at his own cleverness and murmuring, '*Poop! Poop!*'

At the inn he saw a beautiful motor car, whose owners were inside having lunch. Toad could not resist trying it out. He turned the starting handle, hopped in and drove off in a cloud of dust.

Toad's next appearance was as a limp and sorry prisoner in the dock at the magistrate's court. He was charged with dangerous driving, stealing a motor car and, worst of all, cheeking the police. He was sentenced to twenty years' imprisonment.

The wretched Toad was handcuffed and marched across the square to the ancient castle, guarded by men-at-arms and warders. He was dragged through courtyards where bloodhounds strained at their leashes. Down spiralling stone staircases he went, down to the deepest dungeon of all. In front of the heavy

nail-studded door sat an old gaoler
with a mighty bunch of keys.

The unhappy Toad realized what
a foolish animal he had been. He
could never hope to escape from
the best-guarded prison in England.

'What has happened to the clever,
popular Mr Toad, respected by
everybody?' he whimpered. 'O wretched
animal, so justly punished!'

He refused all food and lay limply
on his bed, fat tears rolling down his
flabby cheeks.

CHAPTER SIX

Toad's Escape

THE GAOLER'S DAUGHTER was
a kind young girl who was very fond
of animals. She took pity on Toad and
coaxed him to eat some hot buttered
toast, asking him to tell her all about
Toad Hall. Soon the Toad revived a little
and began to puff himself up and boast
about his home and his possessions.

In spite of his conceit, the young

girl was sorry for him. She hated to see animals shut up. So she thought of a plan to help him to escape. He was to dress in her aunt's clothes.

Her aunt was a washerwoman, who came to the castle once a week. She was short and stout (like Toad!). She wore a long cotton dress, a shawl and an old blue bonnet, and she carried a basket full of washing. Toad did not like the idea of dressing up as a poor old woman, but in the end he agreed.

The gaoler's daughter giggled as she tied the bonnet strings under Toad's chin. 'You look exactly like her!' she laughed (much to Toad's annoyance). 'Goodbye, and good luck! Be careful what you say to the sentries!'

There were some anxious moments as Toad set off, especially as the sentries made rude remarks. But Toad entered into the spirit of the thing, for he fancied

himself as an actor. Soon he came through the prison gate into the sunlight. He was free at last.

He made for the railway station and was about to buy a ticket when he realized he had left his waistcoat, with all his money, in his cell. What could he do now? Then he spotted the engine driver, cleaning down the steam engine.

'Oh, sir,' he cried. 'I'm a poor washerwoman who's lost her purse. How am I to get home, and what will my little children do without me?'

The kind engine driver said, 'Tell you what, missus, I'll give you a ride on my footplate, and you can wash some shirts for me when you get home.'

Toad accepted eagerly and hopped up on the engine. They got up steam and set off. They were soon thudding away down the track, with a trail of white smoke and a whooping whistle.

Suddenly the engine driver looked back. 'There's another train following!' he cried. 'It's full of people – policemen with truncheons – plain-clothes men with bowler hats and umbrellas – prison warders with sticks – all shouting, "*Stop! Stop!*" '

Toad fell on his knees among the coal and begged for help. 'I am not a washerwoman at all,' he confessed. 'I am the well-known daring criminal Mr Toad. Please help me.'

The engine driver hated to see an animal hunted. 'Never mind, I'll help you,' he said. 'When we get through this tunnel, I'll slow down, and you can jump off and hide in the wood.'

They piled on more coal to get up speed, and the sparks flew as they roared through the tunnel. Then they slowed down. Toad jumped off and rolled down the bank into the wood. He laughed as he

saw the other train tear past, full
of policemen and warders, waving
their weapons and shouting, '*Stop!*'

Then he found an old tree and
lay down on a bed of leaves to wait
for morning.

CHAPTER SEVEN

The Further Adventures of Toad

TOAD WAS GETTING nearer and
nearer to home and still had on his
washerwoman's disguise. (By now it
was looking the worse for wear.) Presently
he came to a towpath that ran alongside
a canal. An old horse was plodding
along it, pulling a gaily painted barge.
A stout woman sat in it, her brawny
arm along the tiller.

Toad saw the chance of a lift, so he told his tale of losing a purse and having to get back to his children.

'I'll give you a lift as far as Toad Hall,' the barge-woman said, 'if you'll do my dirty washing for me.' Toad had been boasting what a good washerwoman he was so he could hardly refuse!

The barge-woman gave him a great pile of washing, some soap and clean water in a big tub. Toad had no idea how to set about it. Soon he was puffing and blowing and rubbing and dubbing, but the clothes were no cleaner.

The barge-woman took a closer look at him.

'You're no washerwoman!' she shrieked. 'You're a dirty, ugly toad! Get off my nice clean barge!'

Toad was so annoyed that he jumped off the barge, undid the tow-rope and rode off on the horse, leaving the woman

shaking her fist at him.

He galloped along, thinking how clever he was. By now he was feeling hungry and, as he passed a hedge, the most delicious smell floated over it. A gipsy was cooking a stew in an iron pot on a fire. Quickly Toad struck a bargain. He sold the horse for a few pence and a plate of stew.

He was feeling his old self again and began to make up a boastful song about his adventures:

> '*The world has held great heroes,*
> *As history books have showed,*
> *But never a name to go down to fame*
> *Compared with that of Toad!*'

Suddenly he heard a familiar noise. Along the highway came a motor car – and it was the very one Toad had stolen!

Toad pretended to faint and the car stopped. The passengers took him to be a poor washerwoman and put him in the front seat, where the fresh air would revive him.

Toad soon perked up enough to ask a favour. 'I've always wanted to see if I could drive a motor car,' he said longingly. 'Please let me try!'

The passengers were very amused to think of a humble washerwoman wanting to drive. 'Let her have a go!' they said to the chauffeur.

Toad drove off, slowly at first, then faster.

'Be careful, washerwoman!' they cried.

'I'm not a washerwoman!' said he. 'I'm the great, the famous Toad!' And he drove faster than ever, terrifying the passengers, until he took a corner too fast and drove straight into a pond.

He jumped out and hopped off

across the fields, leaving the passengers standing up to their waists in muddy water. But, when he looked back, he saw the chauffeur and two policemen running after him.

Poor Toad puffed along. He was a very fat animal, and they were gaining on him. What a fool he had been, showing off like that! Suddenly he tripped. He had come to the river bank, and – *splash!* – he fell into the water.

He swam along, gasping, till he came to a hole in the bank. He clutched the edge and looked in.

A small, bright thing shone and moved towards him. A face grew up around it.

Brown and small, with whiskers.

Grave and round, with neat ears.

It was the Water Rat!

CHAPTER EIGHT

The Battle for Toad Hall

WHEN TOAD HAD been dried off and given a suit of Ratty's to wear, Rat told him what had happened while he had been away.

The Wild Wooders had taken over Toad Hall. Weasels, ferrets and stoats were living there, eating Toad's food and drinking his drink and telling everybody that he was never coming back.

Toad was all for going up there at once and turning them out. But Ratty explained that they had armed sentries posted and all the entrances were guarded. He and Badger and Mole patrolled the Hall every day, and there was no way in.

Just then two tired, shabby animals entered. The Badger's clothes were covered with mud.

He said solemnly, 'Welcome home, Toad. Alas, what am I saying? This is a poor homecoming. Unhappy Toad!' And he sat down to eat a piece of cold pie.

But Mole, whose fur was full of bits of hay and straw, danced round Toad joyously and said, 'You must have escaped! O *clever* Toad!'

At this, Toad began to tell all his adventures and show off to the admiring Mole.

'Don't egg him on, Mole,' said Ratty.

'We have to think what to do next.'

They all began to talk at once, until they were silenced by the Badger. 'Be quiet, all of you,' he growled. 'Toad, you bad, troublesome little animal! Aren't you ashamed of yourself? What do you think your father, my old friend, would have said if he'd known of your goings-on?'

Toad rolled over on a sofa and began to sob.

'Never mind that!' said Badger. 'We'll let bygones be bygones. I'll tell you my plan to get Toad Hall back again. There is an underground passage...' And the Badger outlined his plan.

The secret passage came up inside Toad Hall, in the butler's pantry, next to the banqueting hall. That night there was to be a birthday party for the Chief Weasel. Everyone would be in the banqueting hall, except for a few sentries outside in the grounds.

Badger and his men would creep along the tunnel, armed to the teeth, then come up inside the hall and take the Wild Wooders by surprise.

Badger had a pile of weapons, and Ratty set them out in four little heaps. As he ran from one to the other, he muttered busily, 'Here's a sword for the Rat, here's a sword for the Mole, here's a sword for the Toad, here's a sword for the Badger! Here's a pistol for the Rat, here's a pistol for the Mole...' and so on, till all the weapons were sorted out.

Then they had a supper of bacon, beans and macaroni pudding. When it was dark, they put on their belts and pistols and swords and set off. Badger led the way, flourishing a thick stick.

They kept stopping in the darkness, and they bumped into one another several times. This gave Toad, who was lost, quite a fright. But soon they heard

the noise of the feast overhead – the
stamping of little feet, the clinking of
glasses and cheers.

'Now, boys, all together!' said Badger,
and they heaved at the trap door. They
came up into the butler's pantry and
could hear the Chief Weasel giving a
speech of thanks.

'I should like to say a word about
our kind host, Mr Toad,' he sniggered.
'*Good* Toad! *Modest* Toad! *Honest* Toad!'
Everyone laughed.

'In return for his hospitality,' the Chief
Weasel went on, 'I have made up a little
song about him!' He began to sing a
very rude song, all about motor cars
and prison, at the top of his squeaky
little voice.

'Let me get at him!' said Toad.

'*Now!*' cried the Badger, and they
burst into the banqueting hall, brandishing
their weapons.

My! What a squeaking and a squealing and a screeching filled the air!

Terrified weasels dived under the tables. Ferrets rushed madly for the fireplace and got hopelessly stuck in the chimney.

The mighty Badger laid about him with his stick. Mole gave a terrible war cry: 'A Mole! A Mole!' Rat flourished his pistol. Toad, swollen with injured pride, went straight for the Chief Weasel. There were only the four of them, but to the Wild Wooders they seemed like an army.

At last the room was clear, and all the weasels fled squeaking back to the Wild Wood, except for a few Mole had given brooms and aprons and set to tidying up the hall.

CHAPTER NINE

The Wanderer's Return

NEXT DAY, TOAD wanted to give
a banquet to celebrate his homecoming.
He spent the morning making out a
programme, full of songs (by Toad)
and speeches (by Toad).

When his friends saw it, they told him
what they thought. 'You *must* turn over
a new leaf, Toad,' they said, 'and stop
showing off!'

'No speeches?'

'No speeches!'

'Not one little song?'

'Not *one* little song!'

Poor Toad! He had to promise to reform. But up in his bedroom, looking in the mirror, he sang his last little song in praise of himself.

> *'The Toad came home!*
> *There was smashing in of window*
>   *and crashing in of door,*
> *There was chivvying of weasels*
>   *that fainted on the floor,*
> *When the Toad came home!*
> *Bang! Go the drums!*
> *The trumpeters are tooting*
>   *and the soldiers are saluting,*
> *And the cannon they are shooting*
>   *and the motor cars are hooting,*
> *As the hero comes!*
> *Shout hooray!*

And let each one of the crowd
try and shout it very loud,
In honour of an animal
of whom you're justly proud,
For it's Toad's — great — day!'

Toad sang this very loudly, with expression and, when he came to the end, he sang it again.

Then he went quietly downstairs to greet his guests. He refused to take any credit for the victory. 'No, no, it was all Badger's idea. Mole and Rat did most of the fighting,' he said modestly. Mole and Rat looked at each other. This was indeed an altered Toad!

The gaoler's daughter and the engine driver were sent presents and letters of thanks. The barge-woman was sent the value of her horse, though Toad protested. The gipsy was sent nothing, as he had done rather well out of the deal.

The four friends sometimes took
a stroll together in the Wild Wood
of a summer evening. Respectful mother
weasels pointed them out to their young
ones, and told them to behave or the
terrible great grey Badger would get
them. This was somewhat unfair to
Badger who was fond of children. But
it never failed to make them behave.